Tiger Shark

Goblin Shark

Horn Shark

Greenland Shark

Bull Shark

Saw Shark

Blue Shark

Angel Shark

Spiny Dogfish

Frilled Shark

Mako Shark

African Lantern Shark

Leopard Shark

Blacknose Shark

Basking Shark

Bonnethead Shark

Para mi familia: Thanks for keeping me wild.
For Connor: Thanks for being my safe harbor—MCM

For Dad: Thank you for introducing me to the ocean
at the front of your surfboard—DEK

PENGUIN WORKSHOP
An imprint of Penguin Random House LLC, New York

First published in the United States of America by Penguin Workshop,
an imprint of Penguin Random House LLC, New York, 2023

Text copyright © 2023 by Melissa Cristina Márquez
Illustrations copyright © 2023 by Devin Elle Kurtz

Visit us online at penguinrandomhouse.com.

Library of Congress Cataloging-in-Publication Data is available.

Manufactured in China

ISBN 9780593523582   10 9 8 7 6 5 4 3 2 HH

Design by Lynn Portnoff

The publisher does not have any control over and does not assume any responsibility
for author or third-party websites or their content.

Mother of Sharks

BY MELISSA CRISTINA MÁRQUEZ

ILLUSTRATED BY DEVIN ELLE KURTZ

PENGUIN WORKSHOP

The setting sun shimmered against the calm waves as I took one last dip in the silky turquoise waters of la Playita del Condado.

"¡Meli, vamos! ¡Dijiste 'cinco minutos más' hace cinco minutos!" my mami called from the shore.

The only problem was when I had to go home.

"Just five more minutes, ¡te lo prometo!" I exclaimed, fiddling with the necklace my abuela had given me. It was my prized possession.

I spotted the tidal pools
in the distance.

These rocky pools filled
with seawater are sometimes
small, shallow puddles or
huge, deep holes!

I had to make these five
minutes count, so I began to
swim toward them.

As I scrambled onto the rocks, I crouched down to peek through the glass-like surface of the water.

Within the pool was a secret universe of its own: Spiky sea urchins and fuzzy seagrass. Swaying anemones and slow sea slugs. But my favorite critter hid inside a speckled shell.

I carefully picked the shell up and placed it in the palm of my hand to see if anyone was home.

"¡Hola! Is anyone there?" I asked, looking inside.

Two beady eyes of a hermit crab squinted back at me.

"You have a beautiful shell. What shall I name you?" I asked.

"I could just tell you my name," the little crab said.

I yelped, my eyes widening as the crab scuttled around my hand.

"¡Mis amigos me llaman Jaiba!"

"What? How can . . . You can talk?" I whispered, making sure that no one would hear me.

"Of course I can!" Jaiba said proudly. "What kind of crab do you take me for?" He didn't wait for my answer. "I've seen you around here before. What's your name?"

"My name's Melissa," I said, trying to make my heart calm down. "But everyone calls me Meli."

Jaiba stopped pacing and slowly blinked his eyes.

"Encantado de conocerte, Meli," he replied. "Nice to have a name for the girl with the ocean in her heart."

"The what?" I asked, wrinkling my brow in confusion. This surely was a dream.

"Follow me, and I'll show you what I mean."
Jaiba hopped off my palm and disappeared
into the tide pool.

My eyes searched for
his shell, but all I saw was a
reflection of my wet, curly
hair and dark brown eyes
rippling through the water.

Then the tide pool began to bubble . . .

and rumble . . .

Suddenly, I was surrounded by endless bright turquoise. Jaiba and I swam deeper and deeper away from the surface and toward a sprawling underwater city!

Crabs and sea stars scuttled away from me along ancient sandy highways, and schools of fish darted past me as if it were rush hour.

"Jaiba, this is the most amazing thing I've ever seen," I gasped, soaring above the bustling views. "But how am I able to breathe underwater? Or talk to you? Is any of this real?"

"Maybe!" Jaiba said, gliding ahead of me. "Maybe not! You'll just have to dive in further and find out."

My legs kicked harder to catch up to the small cangrejito.

But something started to look off. Just a few moments before, the city was aglow.

Then, a stark color began to stand out: *blanco.*

"Jaiba, where did their colors go?" I asked.

My voice sounded too loud. This part of the reef was ghostly and quiet. Goosebumps covered my body.

"Those coral have been bleached," Jaiba said. "Our planet and oceans are heating up, hurting our home."

"Look!" I said, pointing at something bright green wrapped around the ghostly coral skeleton. "What's that in the distance? Is it alive?"

"That's ghost gear. Nasty stuff that's been left behind," Jaiba explained. "It looks like seaweed from far away, but it's actually a net."

A flash of darkness and a *whoosh* from behind the fishing net startled us. Something big was hidden below.

My heart beat wildly in my chest as I locked eyes with the most beautiful creature I'd ever seen. A giant fish with a sharp, pointed snout and slender body was thrashing amid the plastic covering.

My stomach dropped.

"It's stuck! We have to help!" I exclaimed, watching the creature's blue body swing from side to side in panic. I dove down and started to tug at the net around its fins.

"Almost . . . there," I huffed, pulling with all my might. "Got it!"

The creature swam off in the blink of an eye.

"That was a mako shark," Jaiba said. "They're the fastest sharks in the world."

I couldn't tear my eyes away from the shark's shadow, slowly disappearing. I reached out toward it as bubbles began to blur my vision, and I was pulled into a new world again.

"Jaiba! What are we doing here?! We can't just be in someone's room!" I whispered.

"Don't worry, you're invisible. Nobody can see you except me," he replied matter-of-factly.

"So how many kinds of sharks are out there?" I asked.

"Over five hundred different kinds," Jaiba said. "Great white sharks, whale sharks, tiger sharks, blue sharks, reef sharks, epaulettes.

"These creatures have existed before so many of us—before the dinosaurs even! Each one is special."

Great White Shark

Tiger Shark

Whale Shark

Blue Shark

Reef Shark

Epaulette Shark

THE FOOD CHAIN

"Sharks sit at the top of the food chain, helping control and maintain the numbers of animals below them in the food web," Jaiba continued. "We need sharks to keep our oceans healthy."

"They're incredible," I breathed, eyes wide. "I want to help them."

"Maybe you could become a shark scientist one day!" said Jaiba.

"Maybe," I whispered. I had never seen a shark scientist who looked like me before.

"Can you show me more?" I asked.

Jaiba smiled mischievously and flicked his claw.

"Cannonball!" Jaiba yelled as he tucked his body
into his shell and jumped into the clear water.
I pinched my nose and jumped in after him.

Jaiba motioned at me to follow him. "I
wanted you to meet someone—my friend the
nurse shark."

I dove below the surface where
the sun's warmth could still be
felt, to find the shy nurse shark.

"¡Hola! Mi nombre es Meli," I said, trying not to stare at her unique pebbled pattern and long fins.

The nurse shark stiffened and retreated back into the shadows of the coral.

"Bubbles," Jaiba explained. "Some sharks don't like them."

"How strange," I said. "What else do they not like?"

Without a word, Jaiba flicked his claw again.

"Where are we now?"

"A university library," Jaiba said excitedly, leading us through the maze of books.

"C'mon, I know where we'll find the answers to what you're looking for."

I picked up one book about sharks. Then another.

And my questions grew bigger than ever.

WHAT NEW SPECIES of SHARKS are OUT THERE to be DISCOVERED?

WHAT SHARK SPECIES are the MOST ENDANGERED?

DO DIFFERENT SHARKS HAVE DIFFERENT BEHAVIORS?

ARE LITTLE SHARKS AFRAID OF BIG SHARKS?

WHY are PEOPLE SO AFRAID of SHARKS?

WHY AREN'T THERE MORE SHARK SCIENTISTS THAT LOOK LIKE ME?

"Can people really do this for a job? Study sharks and help protect them?" I asked Jaiba. He nodded and said, "Let me show you someone who does just that."

Jaiba transported us to a theater with cozy red chairs that faced a big shiny stage.

Onstage was a woman with wild, curly hair giving a speech. I looked around at the crowded theater and couldn't believe it: a real-life scientist—and she looked just like me!

"Female researchers, especially those of color, are like female sharks lurking in the darkness," the woman said. "We're here, but no one is paying attention."

"We can't be what we can't see."

I could hear her words echoing in my ears as Jaiba snapped his claw.

"But she's so cool! Who was she?" I pleaded with Jaiba. "Couldn't we stay to hear the end of her speech?"
"Ah, but that was just the beginning," said Jaiba with pride. "People call her

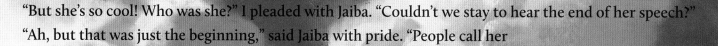
the Mother of sharks.

Her superpower is teaching people to care for sharks around the world."

We watched her ride in a helicopter over the Arctic Ocean on a blizzardy expedition,

and wade the deep waters of Australia to drop underwater cameras and spy on sharks in faraway places, and even deep dive in a yellow submarine!

"¡Qué chévere!" I exclaimed as Jaiba and I followed the
crew of scientists down into the depths of the dark sea.

As we reached the bottom, the Mother of Sharks smiled and shouted, "I see something! To the right!"

A beautiful sixgill shark bumped into the submarine. "We are trying to record the shark's natural behavior so we can learn more about how this animal acts around new objects," she explained to a crew of documentary filmmakers.

I watched as another scientist pulled a small capsule out of a bag.

"Tagging sharks lets scientists track them for a few months!" said Jaiba. "The tag helps gather important information to better protect them."

"This is the coolest thing ever!" I exclaimed.

"It gets cooler." Jaiba laughed from my shoulder.

Instantly, he whisked us off to a boat that was
surrounded by snow, tall mountains, and icebergs.
"Do you see anything yet?" the Mother of Sharks asked.
"We might have something!" another scientist yelled.

"There we go! That's what we're looking for," the Mother of Sharks called out to the rest of the crew. "The largest fish in the Arctic—the Greenland shark!"

The researchers cheered as they quickly let the shark go with a tag attached to track her movements.

"I think they're my new favorite," I told Jaiba loudly, so he could hear me over the cheering scientists.

Suddenly, the Mother of Sharks
locked eyes with *me*.
"Give me a second, amigos," she said
to the group, walking straight toward us.

"I thought you said no one could see me?!"
I whispered nervously to Jaiba.

The sun peeked out from behind the clouds, glinting off the necklace she pulled out from behind her scarf. It was *my* necklace! The one Abuela gave me. A giant smile spread across each of our faces—the same smile.

"I think you've got to get back to the beach, Meli," she finally said as the sun slowly began to set on the horizon.

"That's right! Mami! But there are so many things I want to ask you and Jaiba."

"Good," Jaiba said, pulling me away one last time.

"Keep questioning."

"But what happens now, Jaiba?" I asked as we returned to la Playita del Condado.

"Follow your heart," Jaiba reassured me. "It has the ocean in it, after all. There are always people who want to help sharks. You just have to find them."

"How will I know where to find *you*?" I said, setting Jaiba back down in the tide pool.

"I'm always here. Just look for the speckled shell."

Jaiba winked at me just before a wave crashed into the tidal pool. When the foam disappeared, so did the little critter.

"Han pasado cinco minutos, nos vamos," I heard my mother remind me. Had it only been five minutes? It felt like a lifetime!

"¡Voy, Mami!" I replied.

I looked back at the endless ocean as waves crashed against the glow of the sunset, remembering everything that Jaiba and the Mother of Sharks showed me—

and the world of adventures that lay ahead.

LETTER TO . . . YOU!

Hola!

I wanted to say a big gracias for reading *Mother of Sharks*. My childhood memories of exploring the ocean at la Playita del Condado in San Juan, Puerto Rico, are my favorite ones. I can still picture the colorful marine life, hear the roar of the waves, and remember how little pieces of plastic littered the beach and the seafloor. My childhood friends were the sea creatures on the shorelines, and since then, the ocean has been a constant source of fascination for me.

I love every creature that calls the ocean home, but I especially love sharks. While sharks seem scary to many people, an ocean without sharks is the scariest thing in the world to me. Sharks are important! A healthy ocean needs sharks because they help control and maintain the numbers of animals below them on the food chain, keeping marine life in balance.

No matter where we live, the ocean influences all of us. It provides us with the air we breathe and the food we eat. It even influences our weather. Scientists are working really hard to understand and protect our oceans—but we can't do it alone. It's up to all of us and our communities to protect marine life, too. From using less single-use plastic to joining local beach clean-up efforts to educating yourself with resources, books, or documentaries, we all have a part to play. It may feel like a drop in the bucket at first, but our collective action makes a difference.

Growing up on la Playita del Condado made me want to become a scientist. But often, when I looked around, I noticed that there was no one in the science field that looked like me. That is slowly starting to change. I hope this book not only inspires you to help save our oceans but also encourages you to pursue your dream—and dare to dive deeper into the unknown.

Saludos,
Melissa

GLOSSARY

BLUE SHARK: They are curious predators that live throughout our oceans, from the tropics to temperate waters. Their bluish skin gives them their name and is perfect for blending into the open ocean waters.

EPAULETTE SHARK: Also known as the walking shark, they can walk, both along the seafloor and across land, for short distances thanks to their fins! They are known to survive on very little oxygen while looking for food in tidal pools.

GREAT WHITE SHARK: Found in cool, coastal waters around the world, great whites are the largest predatory fish on earth—and are famous for jumping out of the water!

GREENLAND SHARK: Not only are Greenland sharks one of the largest living species of shark, but they are also the longest-living animals with a backbone and can survive for up to hundreds of years! They are mainly found in cold waters, like the Arctic Ocean.

MAKO SHARK: A very active and powerful shark with a sharply pointed snout, these sharks prefer warmer ocean waters. The mako is the fastest shark, reaching swimming speeds of over forty-five miles per hour!

NURSE SHARK: These slow-moving bottom dwellers are often seen resting in caves or coral reef overhangs during the daytime. A light yellowish-brown to dark brown color, they are one species of shark that does not need to continue swimming in order to breathe.

REEF SHARK: Sharks that spend most of their life on or around reef habitats are known as reef sharks, and there are quite a few different species! They keep order in their coral reef communities, making sure nobody gets out of line.

SIXGILL SHARK: The sixgill shark is a common species of deepwater shark. A large, slow-moving shark, they get their name from the six long gill slits on each side of their head.

TIGER SHARK: Nicknamed the "trash cans of the sea," they aren't picky about what they eat! Usually found in coastal, tropical waters, their name comes from the tiger-like stripes on their sides that fade as they get older.

WHALE SHARK: Whale sharks are the largest shark and fish alive today. This slow-moving, filter-feeding animal is easy to recognize from the hundreds of white spots covering its body. It sort of looks like a starry night!

RESOURCES

MINORITIES IN SHARK SCIENCES (MISS)
A US nonprofit organization that provides community and funding opportunities for women of color who wish to enter the field of shark sciences.

www.misselasmo.org

CONSERVACIÓN CONCIENCIA
A nonprofit organization based in the United States and Puerto Rico, dedicated to environmental research and conservation that promotes sustainable development, including the creation of Puerto Rico's first shark research and conservation program in collaboration with the seafood industry.

www.conservacionconciencia.org

PELAGIOS KAKUNJÁ
A Mexican nonprofit organization created in 2010 by scientists Mauricio Hoyos and James Ketchum with a goal to study and protect sharks and mantas in Mexico.

www.pelagioskakunja.org

GILLS CLUB
Atlantic White Shark Conservancy's STEM-based organization that is dedicated to connecting girls with female scientists globally and aims to inspire shark and ocean conservation.

www.gillsclub.org

THE FINS UNITED INITIATIVE
An organization, founded by Melissa herself, that raises awareness about unusual and diverse sharks (and their relatives) in the world, as well as the diverse scientists who study them.

TRANSLATIONS

"¡Meli, vamos! ¡Dijiste 'cinco minutos más' hace cinco minutos!"
"Meli, let's go! You said 'five more minutes' five minutes ago!"

"¡te lo prometo!"
"I promise you!"

my abuela
my grandmother

"¡Mis amigos me llaman Jaiba!"
"My friends call me Jaiba!"

"Encantado de conocerte, Meli."
"Pleased to meet you, Meli."

cangrejito
little crab

blanco
white

"¡Hola! Mi nombre es Meli."
"Hello! My name is Meli."

"¡Qué chévere!"
"Cool!"

"Han pasado cinco minutos, nos vamos."
"Five minutes have passed, let's go."

"¡Voy, Mami!"
"Coming, Mommy!"

Caribbean Reef Shark

Hammerhead Shark

Zebra Shark

Lemon Shark

Whale Shark

Oceanic Whitetip Shark

Blacktip Reef Shark

Great White Shark

Swell Shark

Thresher Shark

Nurse Shark

Salmon Shark